Let's Enjoy Masterpieces!

# The Little Match Girl

## 賣火柴的小女孩

### The Emperor's Clothes · 國王的新衣
### The Red Shoes · 紅舞鞋

Author　　Hans Christian Andersen
Adaptor　　Louise Benette, David Hwang
Illustrator　Kim Hyeon-Jeong

# Let's Enjoy Masterpieces!

All the beautiful fairy tales and masterpieces that you have encountered during your childhood remain as warm memories in your adulthood. This time, let's indulge in the world of masterpieces through English. You can enjoy the depth and beauty of original works, which you can't enjoy through Chinese translations.

The stories are easy for you to understand because of your familiarity with them. When you enjoy reading, your ability to understand English will also rapidly improve.

This series of *Let's Enjoy Masterpieces* are a special reading comprehension booster program, devised to improve reading comprehension for beginners whose command of English is not satisfactory, or who are elementary, middle, and high school students. With this program, you can enjoy reading masterpieces in English with fun and efficiency.

This carefully planned program is composed of 5 levels, from the beginner level of 350 words to the intermediate and advanced levels of 1,000 words. With this program's level-by-level system, you are able to read famous texts in English and to savor the true pleasure of the world's language.

The program is well conceived, composed of reader-friendly explanations of English expressions and grammar, quizzes to help the student learn vocabulary and understand the meaning of the texts, and fabulous illustrations that adorn every page. In addition, with our "Guide to Listening," not only is reading comprehension enhanced but also listening comprehension skills are highlighted.

In the audio recording of the book, texts are vividly read by professional American actors. The texts are rewritten, according to the levels of the readers by an expert editorial staff of native speakers, on the basis of standard American English with the ministry of education recommended vocabulary. Therefore, it will be of great help even for all the students that want to learn English.

Please indulge yourself in the fun of reading and listening to English through *Let's Enjoy Masterpieces*.

# 安徒生

Hans Christian
Andersen
(1805–1875)

Hans Christian Andersen was born on April 2, 1805, in Odense, a small fishing village on the island of Funen. His father was a poor cobbler. Even so, he was a literary man of progressive ideas, who enjoyed reading and encouraged his son Hans Andersen to cultivate his artistic interests.

Andersen started writing while he was a university student. After his first novel *Improvisatore*, which was based on his trip to Italy in 1833, received critical acclaim, Andersen earned even greater fame as a writer with his first book of fairy tales, *Tales Told for Children*. Later, Anderson became a well-loved writer of children's literature. By the time of his death in 1875, he had published a total of around 130 tales.

Andersen wrote many books that have been considered as the best works of literature for children, such as *The Little Mermaid*, *The Ugly Duckling*, and *The Emperor's New Clothes*. Despite many difficulties, Andersen rose above challenges to become a successful writer. In his works, Anderson zealously intertwined his lyrical writing style with manifestations of beautiful imaginary lands and humanism.

After having lived a solitary life, Andersen died alone in 1875. On his funeral day, all the Danish people wore mourning clothes, and the king and queen attended his funeral. Andersen was also an active poet, and his beautiful fairy tales are still loved by people around the world.

## The Little Match Girl

It was New Year's Eve. A poor little girl was walking down the snow-covered streets. She had not sold one box of matches all day, and she was too frightened to go home, so the poor little match girl sat sadly beside the fountain and took out a match and lit it. She cupped her hand over it, and as she did so, she started to see magical things in its light . . .

Like many of Andersen's tales, *The Little Match Girl* has touched the hearts of children and adults all around the world. The author wrote this story for his mom who had a very poor childhood.

## The Emperor's New Clothes

This was adapted from the story *Duke Rukanore* by J. Manuel, a 14th century Spanish author. Once upon a time, there was an emperor who loved new clothes so much that he spent huge amounts of money on obtaining them. One day, some swindlers convinced the emperor that they could make clothes that would be invisible to any man who was stupid. The original fairy tale is a critical look at society.

## The Red Shoes

A long time ago, there was a little girl who was pretty but poor. She was obliged to go barefooted. Then she bought a pair of new red shoes. However, every time she put on the shoes, she couldn't stop dancing. One day her adoptive mother fell ill, but the little girl did not take care of her. Instead, she put the red shoes on, went to the ball, and began to dance. Strangely enough, she could not take the shoes off and had to dance far out into the dark woods for a couple of days and nights. This story has the strong Christian message: retribution of selfishness.

# HOW TO USE THIS BOOK
## 本書使用說明

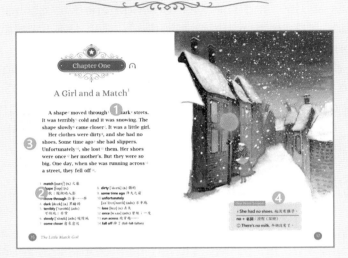

## 1 *Original English texts*

It is easy to understand the meaning of the text, because the text is divided phrase by phrase and sentence by sentence.

## 2 *Explanation of the vocabulary*

The words and expressions that include vocabulary above the elementary level are clearly defined.

## 3 *Response notes*

Spaces are included in the book so you can take notes about what you don't understand or what you want to remember.

## 4 *One point lesson*

In-depth analyses of major grammar points and expressions help you to understand sentences with difficult grammar.

## 🎧 *Audio Recording*

In the audio recording, native speakers narrate the texts in standard American English. By combining the written words and the audio recording, you can listen to English with great ease.

Audio books have been popular in Britain and America for many decades. They allow the listener to experience the proper word pronunciation and sentence intonation that add important meaning and drama to spoken English. Students will benefit from listening to the recording twenty or more times.

After you are familiar with the text and recording, listen once more with your eyes closed to check your listening comprehension. Finally, after you can listen with your eyes closed and understand every word and every sentence, you are then ready to mimic the native speaker.

Then you should make a recording by reading the text yourself. Then play both recordings to compare your oral skills with those of a native speaker.

# HOW TO IMPROVE
# READING ABILITY
## 如何增進英文閱讀能力

### 1 *Catch key words*

Read the key words in the sentences and practice catching the gist of the meaning of the sentence. You might question how working with a few important words could enhance your reading ability. However, it's quite effective. If you continue to use this method, you will find out that the key words and your knowledge of people and situations enables you to understand the sentence.

### 2 *Divide long sentences*

Read in chunks of meaning, dividing sentences into meaningful chunks of information. In the book, chunks are arranged in sentences according to meaning. If you consider the sentences backwards or grammatically, your reading speed will be slow and you will find it difficult to listen to English.

You are ready to move to a more sophisticated level of comprehension when you find that narrowly focusing on chunks is irritating. Instead of considering the chunks, you will make it a habit to read the sentence from the beginning to the end to figure out the meaning of the whole.

### ③ *Make inferences and assumptions*

Making inferences and assumptions are part of your ability. If you don't know, try to guess the meaning of the words. Although you don't know all the words in context, don't go straight to the dictionary. Developing an ability to make inferences in the context is important.

The first way to figure out the meaning of a word is from its context. If you cannot make head or tail out of the meaning of a word, look at what comes before or after it. Ask yourself what can happen in such a situation. Make your best guess as to the word's meaning. Then check the explanations of the word in the book or look up the word in a dictionary.

### ④ *Read a lot and reread the same book many times*

There is no shortcut to mastering English. Only if you do a lot of reading will you make your way to the summit. Read fun and easy books with an average of less than one new word per page. Try to immerse yourself in English as often as you can.

Spend time "swimming" in English. Language learning research has shown that immersing yourself in English will help you improve your English, even though you may not be aware of what you're learning.

# CONTENTS

# The Little Match Girl

## 賣火柴的小女孩

# Before You Read

smoke
煙

chimney
煙囪

New Year's Eve
除夕

Help Yourself.
自己來，不要客氣。

Happy New Year!
新年快樂！

lights
燈火

He is lighting the candles.
他正在點蠟燭。

fireplace
火爐

make a wish
許願

candles
蠟燭

He is smelling the food.
他在聞食物的香味。

goose
鵝肉

dishes
菜餚

feast
大餐

cand
糖果

table cloth
桌布

delicious
美味的

I want to eat the delicious food.
我想吃美味的食物。

**falling star**
流星
She watched one of the stars falling.
她看到一顆流星。

**snowy**
下雪的

**windy**
風大的

The snow is falling.
正在下雪。

The wind is blowing hard.
風很大。

**terribly**
可怕地；非常
It was terribly cold.
冷得要命。

**mittens**
連指手套

**scarf**
圍巾

**coat**
大衣

The old lady is rubbing her hands together.
那個老太太在摩擦雙手。

**icy road**
結冰的道路

**boots**
靴子

**stove**
爐子

It will make my hands warmer.
這會讓我的手暖一些。

**strike**
劃（火柴）

**light**
點燃
She lit a match.
她點了一根火柴。

**a bundle of matches**
一綑火柴

**sparkle like a diamond**
像鑽石一樣閃耀

Her body was like ice.
她的身體冰冷。

**dirty clothes**
髒衣服

**burnt matches**
點過的火柴

**bare feet**
赤腳

# Chapter One

## A Girl and a Match[1]

A shape[2] moved through[3] the dark[4] streets. It was terribly[5] cold and it was snowing. The shape slowly[6] came closer[7]. It was a little girl.

Her clothes were dirty[8], and she had no shoes. Some time ago[9] she had slippers. Unfortunately[10], she lost[11] them. Her shoes were once[12] her mother's. But they were so big. One day, when she was running across[13] a street, they fell off[14].

1. **match** [mætʃ] (n.) 火柴
2. **shape** [ʃeɪp] (n.)
   形狀；模糊的人影
3. **move through** 沿著……移
4. **dark** [dɑːrk] (a.) 黑暗的
5. **terribly** [ˋterəbli] (adv.)
   可怕地；非常
6. **slowly** [ˋslouli] (adv.) 緩慢地
7. **come closer** 愈來愈近
   (come-came-come)
8. **dirty** [ˋdɜːrti] (a.) 髒的
9. **some time ago** 許久之前
10. **unfortunately**
    [ʌnˋfɔːrtʃənɪtli] (adv.) 不幸地
11. **lose** [luːz] (v.) 遺失
    (lose-lost-lost)
12. **once** [wʌns] (adv.) 曾經；一度
13. **run across** 跑穿越……
14. **fall off** 掉了 (fall-fell-fallen)

One Point Lesson

She had **no shoes**. 她沒有鞋子。

**no** + 名詞：沒有（某物）

ex There's **no milk**. 牛奶沒有了。

The snow was falling[1] from the beautiful winter sky. It was New Year's Eve[2]. The streets were almost[3] empty[4] now. Everyone was inside[5] their warm homes.

The little girl walked in the snow with bare[6] feet. In her hands, she was carrying[7] some matches. Every day, she went out to sell[8] matches. But today she didn't sell any[9]. She was so cold but she couldn't go home. When she didn't sell any matches, her father would beat[10] her.

1. **fall** [fɔːl] (v.) 掉落；下
   (fall-fell-fallen)
2. **New Year's Eve** 除夕
3. **almost** [`ɔːlmoust] (adv.) 幾乎
4. **empty** [`empti] (a.) 空的
5. **inside** [ɪn`saɪd]
   (prep.) 在⋯⋯裡面
6. **bare** [ber] (a.) 赤裸的
7. **carry** [`kæri] (v.) 攜帶
8. **sell** [sel] (v.) 賣
   (sell-sold-sold)
9. **not . . . any** 一點都沒有
10. **beat** [biːt] (v.) 打
    (beat-beat-beaten)

*The Little Match Girl*

One Point Lesson

Every day, she went out **to sell** matches.
她每天都出去賣火柴。

**to** ＋原形動詞：在動詞（went）後面的動詞要用不定詞
（to ＋ 原形動詞）。

ex He went out **to buy** some bread. 他出去買麵包。

"Oh! I am so hungry," she said. "I want to eat something. I am so cold too," she thought.

She walked past[1] some houses. Through[2] the windows, she could see bright[3] lights[4] shining[5]. Then, she smelled some meat[6] roasting[7]. It was painful[8] to her. She was so hungry.

"I want to eat that delicious[9] meat," she thought. "So many people are spending[10] a wonderful[11] time with their families. They are eating wonderful food."

1. **past** [pæst] (prep.) 經過
2. **through** [θruː] (prep.) 穿過；透過
3. **bright** [braɪt] (a.) 明亮的
4. **light** [laɪt] (n.) 亮光；燈光
5. **shine** [ʃaɪn] (v.) 發光 (shine-shone-shone)
6. **meat** [miːt] (n.) 肉
7. **roast** [roʊst] (v.) 烤
8. **painful** [ˋpeɪnfəl] (a.) 痛苦的
9. **delicious** [dɪˋlɪʃəs] (a.) 美味的
10. **spend** [spend] (v.) 花費 (spend-spent-spent)
11. **wonderful** [ˋwʌndərfəl] (a.) 精彩的；很棒的

Through the windows, she could **see** bright lights **shining**.
透過窗戶，她可以看到燦爛的亮光。

She **smelled** some meat **roasting**.
她聞到烤肉的香味。

---

**see / smell + 動詞 + -ing**：感官動詞（see, smell, hear . . .）後面的動詞加 -ing，表示看到（聞到、聽到……）當時正在進行的動作。

ex I **hear** the children **laughing**. 我聽到孩子們在笑。

🎧 4

On this terrible day, she found[1] a corner[2] and sat down. She tried to warm[3] herself. But she only[4] became[5] colder. Her body was like[6] ice. She rubbed[7] her hands together to make them warm. It was useless[8].

"Ah! The matches," she thought. "Just one! It will make my hands warmer."

She took one match and struck[9] it against[10] the wall. She was amazed[11].

"Oh, it is so beautiful!" she thought.

She felt the warmth[12] from that one tiny[13] match.

---

1. **find** [faɪnd] (v.) 找到；發現
   (find-found-found)
2. **corner** [ˋkɔːrnə(r)] (n.) 角落
3. **warm** [wɔːrm] (a.) 溫暖的
4. **only** [ˋoʊnli] (adv.) 只是
5. **become** [bɪˋkʌm] (v.) 變成
   (become-became-become)
6. **like** [laɪk] (prep.) 如；好像
7. **rub** [rʌb] (v.) 摩擦
   (rub-rubbed-rubbed)
8. **useless** [ˋjuːsləs]
   (a.) 無用的
9. **strike** [straɪk] (v.)
   劃（火柴）；打擊
   (strike-struck-struck)
10. **against** [əˋgenst] (prep.) 靠著
11. **amazed** [əˋmeɪzd] (a.) 吃驚的
12. **warmth** [wɔːrmθ] (n.) 溫暖
13. **tiny** [ˋtaɪni] (a.) 微小的

*The Little Match Girl*

One Point Lesson

She rubbed her hands together to make them warm.
她摩擦雙手，讓手溫暖。

make A B：使 A 變得 B。A 是受詞，B 是形容詞。

ex This scarf will keep you warm. 這條圍巾可以使你溫暖。

◊ **In her hand** was the burnt match.
　她手上的是已點過的火柴。

___

**倒裝句**：將句子副詞片語（in her hand）放在句首，並將主詞
　　　　放在動詞後面，這樣的句子就是倒裝句，目的是為了強
　　　　調。正常語序為：The burnt match was in her hand.

**ex** **Here** comes the bus. 公車來了。

5

Suddenly[1], everything became very strange[2]. The little girl was in a new place. There was a large stove[3] in front of[4] her.

"What is this?" she asked. "This stove is so warm."

She felt the warmth from that wonderful stove.

"I want to stay[5] here forever[6]."

She put her hands closer to the stove. In a flash[7], everything was gone[8]. She looked at her hand. In her hand was the burnt[9] match. She felt very disappointed[10].

1. **suddenly** [`sʌdənli]
   (adv.) 忽然地
2. **strange** [streɪndʒ]
   (a.) 奇怪的
3. **stove** [stoʊv] (n.) 爐子
4. **in front of** 在……前面
5. **stay** [steɪ] (v.) 留下來
6. **forever** [fər`evə(r)]
   (adv.) 永遠
7. **in a flash** 一瞬間
8. **be gone** 消失了
9. **burnt** [bɜːrnt] (a.) 燒過的
10. **disappointed**
    [ˌdɪsə`pɔɪntɪd] (a.) 失望的

## Comprehension Quiz Chapter One

### A Fill in the blanks to complete the vocabulary.

1. very small ⇨ t ___ ___ ___
2. not clean ⇨ d ___ ___ ___ ___
3. nothing inside ⇨ e ___ ___ ___ ___
4. not cold but not very hot ⇨ w ___ ___ ___

### B Fill in the blanks with the given words.

stove sell gone bare rubbed

1. Every day the little match girl went out to ________ matches.
2. She walked in the snow with ________ feet.
3. She ________ her hands together to make them warm.
4. She struck a match against the wall and saw a large ________.
5. The match went out and everything was ________.

## C Fill in the blanks according to the story.

**1** She looked at her hand. In her hand was the burnt _____.

**2** She found a _____ and sat down.

**3** She took one _____ and struck it against the wall.

**4** She felt the warmth from the one tiny _____.

## D Choose the correct answer.

**1** Why didn't the little match girl go home?

(a) Because she didn't have a house.

(b) Because she lost her way.

(c) Because her father would beat her.

**2** What happened to the little girl's shoes?

(a) Someone stole them.

(b) She lost them.

(c) They became too small for her.

# Chapter Two

# Journey[1] to Paradise[2]

"I will light[3] another match," she thought. "Maybe[4] the stove will come again[5]."

Again, the match sparkled[6] like a diamond in the cold night air[7]. This time was very different. She could see a wonderful room.

"Oh, how wonderful it is!" she cried out[8].

There was elegant[9] furniture[10]. On the table was an amazing[11] feast[12]. In the middle[13] was a big goose[14]. The smell was mouth-watering[15].

1. **journey** [`dʒɜːrni] (n.) 旅程
2. **paradise** [`pærədaɪs] (n.) 天堂
3. **light** [laɪt] (v.) (light-lit-lit) 點燃
4. **maybe** [`meɪbi] (adv.) 或許
5. **come again** 再來
6. **sparkle** [`spɑːrkḷ] (v.) 發光；閃耀
7. **in the air** 在空中
8. **cry out** 大喊 (cry-cried-cried)

9. **elegant** [`ɛləgənt] (a.) 精緻的
10. **furniture** [`fɜːrnɪtʃə(r)] (n.) 家具
11. **amazing** [ə`meɪzɪŋ] (a.)
    驚人的；令人驚奇的
12. **feast** [fiːst] (n.) 大餐；筵席
13. **in the middle** 在中間

14. **goose** 鵝 [guːs] (n.)
    （複數形 geese [giːs]）
15. **mouth-watering**
    [`maυθˌwɑːtərɪŋ]
    (a.) 令人流口水的

🎧 7

The little girl watched all of this.

"I want to eat the delicious food," she thought. "I want to sit[1] in the elegant chairs."

Suddenly the goose rolled toward[2] the poor little girl. She tried to[3] get[4] it, but it all disappeared[5]. There was nothing left[6] but[7] the burnt match.

Without thinking, she took another match and lit it. She wanted to see that wonderful sight[8] again.

    This time⁹, she was sitting under the most amazing Christmas tree. This scene was so much better¹⁰ than any of the others¹¹.

1. **sit** [sɪt] (v.) 坐下 (sit-sat-sat)
2. **roll toward** 滾向
3. **try to** 試著去
4. **get** [ɡet] (v.) 拿 (get-got-got)
5. **disappear** [ˌdɪsə`pɪr] (v.) 消失
6. **leave** [liːv] (v.) 留下；剩下 (leave-left-left)
7. **but** [bʌt] (prep.) 除了⋯⋯之外
8. **sight** [saɪt] (n.) 景象
9. **this time** 這次
10. **better** [`betə(r)] (a.) 更好的 (good 的比較級)
11. **than any other** 比其他的

She wanted to touch[1] one of the candles[2]. She lifted[3] her hands toward the tree, but all the candles rose[4] higher and higher[5]. The candles became the stars. She watched one of them falling. It made[6] a fiery[7] line in the sky.

The little girl then thought of[8] her grandmother. Her granny[9] died[10] many years ago. She was the only person who was kind to the little girl.

"A person is dying somewhere[11]," she whispered[12]. "Granny told me that. When a star falls through the sky, the person's soul[13] goes up to heaven[14]."

1. **touch** [tʌtʃ] (v.) 碰觸
2. **candle** [ˋkændl] (n.) 蠟燭
3. **lift** [lɪft] (v.) 舉起
4. **rise** [raɪz] (v.) 升起；上升
   (rise-rose-risen)
5. **higher and higher** 愈來愈高
6. **make** (v.) 產生
   (make-made-made)
7. **fiery** [ˋfaɪəri] (a.) 火一般的
8. **think of** 想起
9. **granny** [ˋgræni] (n.) 奶奶
10. **die** [daɪ] (v.) 死
11. **somewhere** [ˋsʌmwer] (adv.) 在某處
12. **whisper** [ˋwɪspə(r)] (v.) 低聲說出
13. **soul** [soʊl] (n.) 靈魂
14. **heaven** [ˋhevən] (n.) 天堂

 9

She felt [1] very sad. She missed [2] her grandmother very much. She immediately [3] lit another [4] match. It was brighter than all of the other matches.

She watched the center [5] of the light. Slowly, the shape of her grandmother appeared [6]. Her face looked so gentle [7] and kind.

1. **feel** [fiːl] (v.) 感覺
   (feel-felt-felt)
2. **miss** [mɪs] (v.) 想念
3. **immediately** [ɪˋmiːɪtli]
   (adv.) 立即地
4. **another** [əˋnʌðə(r)] (a.) 另一個
5. **center** [ˋsentə(r)] (n.) 中央
6. **appear** [əˋpɪr] (v.) 出現
7. **gentle** [ˋdʒentl] (a.) 溫和
8. **without** [wɪˋðaʊt] (prep.) 沒有
9. **take** 帶走 (take-took-taken)
10. **go out** 熄滅
11. **leave** [liːv] (v.) 離開
    (leave-left-left)

"Granny!" she cried out. "I miss you so much. I am so sad without[8] you. Please take[9] me with you. Don't disappear when the match goes out[10]. I don't want you to leave[11] me again."

**One Point Lesson**

◉ I don't want you to leave me again.
　我不要你再離開我了。

---

**want + somebody + to + V：要某人做事。**

ex He **wanted me to go** with him.
　他要我跟他一起走。

Then the little girl had an idea. She lit the rest[1] of the matches. The matches shone so brightly[2].

The grandmother took the little girl in her arms. The little girl felt safe[3] with her grandmother now. They flew[4] higher and higher into the air[5]. The grandmother took the little girl to paradise.

In that place, the girl never[6] felt cold again. She never felt hungry or sad again. She could live happily[7] with her loving[8] grandmother.

1. **rest** [rest] (n.) 其餘的東西
2. **brightly** [ˋbraɪtlɪ]
   (adv.) 明亮地
3. **safe** [seɪf] (a.) 安全的
4. **fly** [flaɪ] 飛 (fly-flew-flown)
5. **into the air** 到天空
6. **never** [ˋnɛvə(r)] (adv.) 從不
7. **happily** [ˋhæpəlɪ]
   (adv.) 快樂地
8. **loving** [ˋlʌvɪŋ] (a.) 慈愛的

**A** Fill in the blanks with the given words.

> candle    disappear    heaven    delicious

**1** _____ food tastes very nice.

**2** If something _____, you cannot see it anymore.

**3** A _____ gives light.

**4** Some people believe that they will go to _____ when they die.

**B** True or False.

T F   **1** The little girl ate a turkey on a beautiful table.

T F   **2** She saw a Christmas tree and candles.

T F   **3** She touched some of the candles.

T F   **4** Her granny was very nice to the little girl.

T F   **5** The light went out and her granny disappeared.

# The Emperor's New Clothes

## 國王的新衣

# Before You Read

A long time ago, there lived an emperor.
很久以前，有一個皇帝

mirror
鏡子

emperor
皇帝

crown
皇冠

look into the mirror
照鏡子

coat
外套

vest
背心

cloak
斗篷

shirt
襯衫

train
下擺

underwear /
underclothes
內衣 / 貼身衣物

The emperor isn't
wearing any clothes.
皇帝沒穿衣服。

pants
褲子

It looks very good on you,
Your Majesty.
你穿起來很好看，陛下。

undress
把衣服脫掉

stockings
長襪

new clothes
新衣

shoes
鞋子

change his clothes
換衣服

feather
羽毛

dress up
裝扮

put on his hat
戴上他的帽子

get dressed
穿衣

40

# Chapter One

🎧 11 # Two Thieves[1]

A long time ago, there lived an emperor[2]. The emperor's love was his clothes[3]. Every day, he wore[4] the finest[5] clothes. He often[6] changed a few times[7] a day. His purpose[8] was always to show off[9] his clothes. When he

1. **thief** [θiːf] (n.) 小偷
   （複數形：thieves）
2. **emperor** [`empərə(r)] (n.) 皇帝
3. **clothes** [klovz] (n.) 衣服
4. **wear** [wer] (v.) 穿
   (wear-wore-worn)
5. **finest** [`faɪnəst] (a.) 最好的
   （fine 的最高級）

6. **often** [`ɔːfn] (adv.) 經常地
7. **a few times** 好幾次
8. **purpose** [`pɜːrpəs] (n.) 目的
9. **show off** 炫耀
10. **country** [`kʌntri] (n.) 國家
11. **care about** 關心
12. **plan** [plæn] (n.) 計劃
13. **deceive** [dɪ`siːv] (v.) 欺騙
14. **pretend** [prɪ`tend] (v.) 假裝
15. **magic** [`mædʒɪk] (a.) 有魔力的
16. **cloth** [klɔːθ] (n.) 布

met people from other countries [10], he cared only about [11] his clothes.

Two thieves heard about this emperor. They thought of a plan [12] to deceive [13] the emperor.

"Let's go to the city. We can pretend [14] we can make magic [15] cloth [16]," one of the thieves said.

One Point Lesson

◦ He **often** changed a few times a day.
他經常一天要換好幾次衣服。

**often**：表示頻率多寡的頻率副詞，包括 always、
　　　　sometimes 等，通常放在所修飾的動詞前面。

ex I **sometimes** go to school by bus.
我有時會搭公車上學。

🎧 12

The two thieves arrived in[1] the city.

"We are able to[2] make magic cloth. Fools[3] cannot see the cloth," they said.

Soon, everyone knew of the magic cloth. The emperor also heard about it.

1. **arrive in** 抵達
2. **be able to** 可以
3. **fool** [fuːl] (n.) 傻瓜
4. **wise** [waɪz] (a.) 聰明的
5. **made from** 由⋯⋯做的
6. **smart** [smɑːrt] (a.) 聰明的
7. **stupid** [ˋstuːpɪd] (a.) 愚笨的
8. **advisor** [ədˋvaɪzə(r)] (n.) 顧問

"Magic cloth!" he thought. "Only wise[4] men can see this cloth. And people say it is very beautiful. If I have clothes made from[5] this cloth, then I will know who is smart[6] and who is stupid[7]. I will know which of my advisors[8] are wise."

### One Point Lesson

If I have clothes made from this cloth, then I will know who is smart and who is stupid. 如果我有這塊布做成的衣服,我就可以知道誰聰明,誰愚笨。

---

條件句 If . . . + will / can / may + 原形動詞:
如果……,就要/可以/能……。

ex If I see him today, I will ask him to help me.
我今天如果看到他,我會叫他幫我。

🎧 13

    The emperor called¹ the two deceivers² to his palace³. "Can you make me the finest clothes with the magic cloth?" the emperor asked them.

    "Oh, yes! Of course, Your Majesty⁴. But we will need a lot of money, silk⁵, and gold thread⁶."

1. **call** [kɔːl] (v.) 叫；召喚
2. **deceiver** [dɪˋsiːvə(r)] (n.) 騙子
3. **palace** [ˋpælɪs] (n.) 皇宮
4. **Majesty** [ˋmædʒɪsti] (n.)（大寫）陛下
5. **silk** [sɪlk] (n.) 絲

6. **thread** [θred] (n.) 線
7. **loom** [luːm] (n.) 織布機
8. **weave** [wiːv] (v.) 編織（weave-wove-woven）
9. **sew** [soʊ] (v.) 縫（sew-sewed-sewn）

*The Emperor's New Clothes*

The emperor gave them everything they needed.

They quickly started making the magic cloth. They sat at their looms[7] and pretended to weave[8]. They moved their arms as if they were sewing[9].

## 14

After a few days, the emperor became[1] very curious[2].

"I wonder[3] what my clothes are like," he thought.

He called one of his advisors and said, "I want you to go and see my new clothes. Come back quickly[4] and tell me how they look."

The advisor entered[5] the room and told the two thieves, "I have come to see the emperor's new clothes."

"Yes, yes," they said eagerly[6]. "Come this way."

They pretended to hold[7] up some cloth.

"What do you think? Isn't it beautiful?" they asked.

1. **become** [bɪ`kʌm] (v.) 變得 (become-became-become)
2. **curious** [`kjʊriəs] (a.) 好奇的
3. **wonder** [`wʌndə(r)] (v.) 懷疑；納悶
4. **quickly** [`kwɪkli] (adv.) 很快地
5. **enter** [`entə(r)] (v.) 進入
6. **eagerly** [`i:gərli] (adv.) 熱切地
7. **hold** [hoʊld] (v.) 抓住；握著 (hold-held-held)

**One Point Lesson**

🔸 **I have come** to see the emperor's new clothes.
　我是來看皇帝的新衣服的。

---

**完成式**：Have + 動詞的過去分詞→表示動作已經完成。

**ex** I **have finished** my homework.
　我已經寫完我的家庭作業了。

One Point Lesson

It is the finest fabric I **have ever seen**.
這是我所見過最棒的布料。

---

最高級與 ever、never、before 連用，表示強調。

ex This is the best food I **have ever eaten**.
這是我吃過最棒的食物。

15

The advisor was shocked[1]. He couldn't see anything. He was very worried[2].

"Am I stupid?" he thought to himself[3]. "Nobody must know that I cannot see the cloth."

"Ah, yes. It is . . . it is very beautiful," he said in a very nervous[4] voice[5]. "The colors are splendid[6]. The emperor will be very happy."

The advisor returned[7] to the emperor and said, "It is the finest fabric[8] I have ever seen. You will be delighted[9] with it."

1. **shocked** [ʃɑːkt] (a.) 震驚的
2. **worried** [ˋwɜːrid] (a.) 擔心的
3. **think to oneself** 心裡想
4. **nervous** [ˋnɜːrvəs] (a.) 緊張的
5. **voice** [vɔɪs] (n.) 聲音
6. **splendid** [ˋsplendɪd] (a.) 燦爛的
7. **return** [rɪˋtɜːrn] (v.) 返回
8. **fabric** [ˋfæbrɪk] (n.) 布料
9. **delighted** [dɪˋlaɪtɪd] (a.) 欣喜的；高興的

A Crosswords.

B True or False.

T F ❶ The emperor's greatest passion was his clothes.

T F ❷ The two bad men said only fools could see the magic cloth.

T F ❸ The two bad men pretended to work at a loom to make invisible cloth.

T F ❹ The advisor could see the cloth.

**C** Fill in the blanks with the given words.

wise   stupid   finest

1 The emperor wore the _____ clothes.

2 Only _____ men can see this cloth.

3 The two bad men thought, "They are the most _____ people in the world."

**D** Rearrange the following sentences in chronological order.

1 The emperor became curious about his new clothes.

2 Two men went to the city to deceive the emperor.

3 The emperor gave the two men money, silk and gold thread.

4 The advisor pretended to see the invisible cloth.

5 The emperor asked the two men to make him some new clothes.

_____ ⇨ _____ ⇨ _____ ⇨ _____ ⇨ _____

# Chapter Two

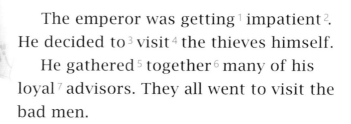

## 🎧 16 The Emperor Wears the New Clothes

The emperor was getting [1] impatient [2]. He decided to [3] visit [4] the thieves himself.

He gathered [5] together [6] many of his loyal [7] advisors. They all went to visit the bad men.

1. **get + 形容詞** 變得……
2. **impatient** [ɪmˈpeɪʃənt] (a.) 不耐煩；沒有耐
3. **decide to** 決定去……
4. **visit** [ˈvɪzɪt] (v.) 拜訪
5. **gather** [ˈgæðə(r)] (v.) 聚集
6. **together** [təˈgeðə(r)] (adv.) 一起
7. **loyal** [ˈlɔɪəl] (a.) 忠誠的
8. **excited** [ɪkˈsaɪtɪd] (a.) 興奮的
9. **terrible** [ˈterəbəl] (a.) 恐怖的；可怕的
10. **feeling** [ˈfiːlɪŋ] (n.) 感覺
11. **pass over** 傳到

Before entering the room, the emperor was very excited[8]. Now, he looked and looked but he couldn't see anything.

A terrible[9] feeling[10] passed over[11] him. "I can't see anything. Am I stupid? I must be. But my advisors must never know I cannot see the clothes."

🎧 17

The emperor suddenly exclaimed [1], "This cloth is the most beautiful one I have ever seen. Weavers [2]! Please hurry [3] to finish [4] the new clothes. I wish to [5] wear them soon."

All of the advisors nodded [6] their heads and said, "Yes, it is beautiful. It will look very good on you, Your Majesty."

4. **finish** [ˋfɪnɪʃ] (v.) 完成
5. **wish to** 希望；但願
6. **nod** [nɑːd] (v.) 點頭 (nod-nodded-nodded)
7. **be pleased with** 對……很滿意
8. **thread** [θred] (n.) 線
9. **alone** [əˋloʊn] (a.) 單獨的

1. **exclaim** [ɪkˋskleɪm] (v.) 驚叫
2. **weaver** [ˋwiːvə(r)] (n.) 織布工
3. **hurry** [ˋhɜːri] (v.) 趕緊

"We are so happy you are pleased with[7] it,"
the two bad men said.

"We will work hard to make the most
beautiful clothes. Also, we need more money,
silk and gold thread[8]."

When they were alone[9], the two men
laughed and laughed.

18

Eventually[1] the two men said, "It is finished."

The emperor was very happy and went to see his new clothes. The two bad men were standing with their arms in the air[2]. They looked like[3] they were holding something up. Of course there was nothing there.

"Aren't they marvelous[4]? They are extremely[5] light[6]. In fact[7], you may even[8] think that you aren't wearing anything," they said.

The emperor undressed[9] and the two thieves pretended to put the clothes on[10] him.

1. **eventually** [ə`ventʃuəli]
   (adv.) 最後；終於
2. **in the air** 在空中
3. **look like** 看起來像是
4. **marvelous** [`mɑːrvələs] (a.)
   了不起的；令人驚歎的
5. **extremely** [ɪk`striːmli]
   (adv.) 非常地；極其
6. **light** [laɪt] (a.) 輕盈的
7. **in fact** 事實上
8. **even** [`iːvən] (adv.) 甚至
9. **undress** [ʌn`drɛs]
   (v.) 脫掉衣服
10. **put on** 穿上

**One Point Lesson**

♦ You may even think **that** you aren't wearing anything.
你甚至可能會以為你沒穿衣服。

---

That：that 在此處是連接詞，用來引導 think 後面所接的子句。

ex His dream was **that** she fell in love with him.
他的夢想是希望她能愛上他。

🎧 19

The emperor turned round[1] and round in front of the mirror[2] and said, "These are the most comfortable[3] clothes I have ever worn. I love this new suit[4]."

All of the attendants[5] agreed[6]. Of course, they could only see his underclothes[7]!

1. **turn round** 轉身
2. **mirror** [ˋmɪrə(r)] (n.) 鏡子
3. **comfortable** [ˋkʌmfətəbl] (a.) 舒服的
4. **suit** [suːt] (n.)（一套）衣服
5. **attendant** [əˋtendənt] (n.) 隨從；侍從
6. **agree** [əˋgriː] (v.) 同意

*The Emperor's New Clothes*

That day, there was to[8] be a special[9] ceremony[10]. Everyone prepared for[11] the ceremony. His attendants pretended to pick up[12] the long train[13] at the back of his cloak[14]. The emperor walked very proudly[15].

7. **underclothes** [ˋʌndərkloʊðz] (n.) 內衣
8. **be to** 將要
9. **special** [ˋspeʃəl] (a.) 特別的
10. **ceremony** [ˋserɪmənɪ] (n.) 儀式；慶典
11. **prepare for** 為了⋯⋯而準備
12. **pick up** 拿起
13. **train** [treɪn] (n.) 下擺
14. **cloak** [kloʊk] (n.) 斗篷；披風
15. **proudly** [ˋpraʊdlɪ] (adv.) 驕傲地

The people in the streets watched and called out[1], "The clothes are beautiful! The emperor looks wonderful!"

Then, a little child in the crowd[2] said, "Daddy, the emperor isn't wearing any[3] clothes."

All the people saw each other's[4] faces. Everyone realized[5] there were no clothes.

In the crowd, there was whispering[6], "The

emperor isn't wearing any clothes."

The emperor could hear all of them. He started to feel very embarrassed[7]. Truly[8], there were no clothes.

After that day, no one spoke of[9] the emperor's new clothes again. Also, the emperor became very humble[10] about his clothes.

1. **call out** 大聲叫喊
2. **crowd** [kraʊd] (n.) 群眾
3. **not . . . any** 沒有任何
4. **each other** 彼此；互相
5. **realize** [ˋriːəlaɪz]
   (v.) 了解；明白
6. **whispering** [ˋwɪspərɪŋ]
   (n.) 耳語；低語
7. **embarrassed** [ɪmˋbærəst]
   (a.) 不好意思的
8. **truly** [ˋtruːli] (adv.) 真實地
9. **speak of** 說起；提到
10. **humble** [ˋhʌmbəl]
    (a.) 謙恭的

## A Choose the correct answer.

① The emperor became very (patient / impatient).

② When the emperor entered the room, he was very (exciting / excited).

③ The clothes were (extreme / extremely) light.

④ The emperor walked (proud / proudly).

## B Rearrange the sentences in chronological order.

① There was a special ceremony.

② The two men pretended to put the clothes on the emperor.

③ The emperor went to see his new clothes.

④ The emperor became very humble about his clothes.

⑤ Everybody realized there were no clothes.

_____ ⇨ _____ ⇨ _____ ⇨ _____ ⇨ _____

# The Red Shoes

## 紅舞鞋

# Before You Read

**inside the church**
教堂裡

**ceiling**
天花板

**devil**
魔鬼

**evil**
邪惡

**angel**
天使

> Dance, you wicked girl.
> 跳吧，妳這個邪惡的女孩。

**dressed in white**
身穿白衣

**confirmation**
堅信禮

**outside the church**
教堂外

**cross**
十字架

**bell**
鐘

**pipe organ**
管風琴

**parson**
教區牧師

**carriage**
馬車

**churchyard**
教堂庭院

**candles**
蠟燭

**dove**
鴿子

It is very bad of you to wear red shoes to church.
妳真是太壞了，竟然穿紅鞋來教堂。

**village people**
村民

**forgive**
原諒

**a selfish girl**
自私的女孩

**neighbor**
鄰居

> God, please forgive me!
> 上帝，請原諒我。

**pray**
禱告

She is praying to God.
她在向上帝禱告。

**mercy**
慈悲；憐憫

Please have mercy on me.
請憐憫我。

**wooden feet**
木頭做的腳

**a feeling of peace and joy**
平安喜樂的感覺

**the Bible**
聖經

### grab
抓；握
She grabbed the
handle of the door.
她抓住門把。

### scold
責罵
The old lady scolded Karen.
那個老太太罵了凱倫。

### receive
收到
She received an
invitation to a ball.
她收到舞會邀請函。

### beg
懇求
She begged to the parson.
她向教區牧師懇求。

### touch
She touched the red shoes.
她摸了紅鞋。

### kick
She kicked the ball.
她踢了踢球。

### cut
剪；切
She cut the paper.
她把紙剪開。

### put on
穿上
She put on the shoes.
她穿上鞋子。

### take off
脫掉
She took off the shoes.
她脫下鞋子。

**shoes**
鞋子

**high-heeled shoes**
高跟鞋

**boots**
靴子

**sandals**
涼鞋

**sneakers**
球鞋

**slippers**
拖鞋

# Chapter One

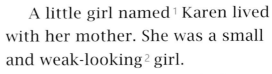 A Poor Little Girl

A little girl named[1] Karen lived with her mother. She was a small and weak-looking[2] girl.

In summer she never had any shoes because she was very poor. In winter she had to[3] wear[4] a pair of[5] heavy[6] wooden[7] shoes.

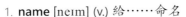

1. **name** [neɪm] (v.) 給……命名
2. **weak-looking** [`wiːk`lʊkɪŋ] (a.) 外表虛弱的
3. **had to** 必須
4. **wear** [wer] (v.) 穿 (wear-wore-worn)
5. **a pair of** 一雙
6. **heavy** [`hevi] (a.) 厚重的
7. **wooden** [`wʊdən] (a.) 木頭的
8. **hurt** [hɜːrt] (v.) 受傷；痛 (hurt-hurt-hurt)
9. **anything else** 任何其他的東西
10. **shoemaker** [`ʃuːˌmeɪkə(r)] (n.) 鞋匠
11. **village** [`vɪlɪdʒ] (n.) 村莊
12. **feel sorry for . . .** 對……感到難過

These shoes always made her feet hurt[8]. But she didn't have anything else[9] to wear.

An old shoemaker[10] in the village[11] felt sorry for[12] her and made a pair of red shoes for her.

They weren't very good shoes, but they made her very happy.

🎧 22

Unfortunately[1], the little girl's mother died[2] soon after[3]. Her mother's funeral[4] was the first time she wore her new shoes. Karen was walking behind[5] her mother's coffin[6].

Just then a large carriage[7] passed by[8]. An old lady in the carriage saw the little girl. She immediately felt sorry for her.

1. **unfortunately**
   [ʌn`fɔːrtʃənɪtli]
   (adv.) 不幸地
2. **die** [daɪ] (v.) 死

3. **soon after** 不久之後
4. **funeral** [`fjuːnərəl] (n.) 喪禮
5. **behind** [bɪ`haɪnd]
   (prep.) 在……之後

To the church minister[9] she said, "Give her to me. I will raise[10] and take care of[11] her."

Karen thought it was all because of[12] the red shoes. But the old lady said, "Those shoes are terrible. Throw them out[13]."

6. **coffin** [`kɔ:fɪn]
   (n.) 棺木；靈柩
7. **carriage** [`kærɪdʒ] (n.) 馬車
8. **pass by** 經過
9. **minister** [`mɪnɪstə(r)]
   (n.) 牧師
10. **raise** [reɪz] (v.) 撫養
11. **take care of** 照顧
12. **because of** 因為
13. **throw out** 丟掉

1. **dress** [drɛs] (v.) 穿著打扮
2. **learn** [lɜːrn] (v.) 學習
3. **travel** [ˋtrævl] (v.) 旅行
4. **daughter** [ˋdɔːtə(r)] (n.) 女兒
5. **crowd around** 圍觀；聚集
6. **nearby** [ˋnɪrˌbaɪ] (a.) 附近的
7. **castle** [ˋkæsəl] (n.) 城堡
8. **through** [θruː]
   (prep.) 穿過；通過
9. **princess** [ˋprɪnsɛs] (n.) 公主
10. **remember** [rɪˋmɛmbə(r)]
   (v.) 記得

23

Karen went to live with the old lady. Every day, she dressed[1] and ate well. She learned[2] many things. She became a very pretty girl.

One day, the queen was traveling[3] with her daughter[4]. All of the village people crowded around[5] the nearby[6] castle[7] to see them. Karen was there, too.

Through[8] a window, she could see the princess[9]. She was dressed in white and wore a beautiful pair of red shoes. Then, Karen remembered[10] her old red shoes.

**One Point Lesson**

● She was dressed in white and wore a beautiful pair of red shoes. 她身穿白衣，並穿了一雙紅鞋。

in white：in + 顏色，表示穿某種顏色的衣服。

ex Here comes a woman in black.
有一位身穿黑衣的女人來了。

## 24

Karen grew older and it was time for her to be confirmed[1]. She needed some new clothes and shoes for this.

In a shop, Karen found some red shoes like the princess's. But she needed to wear black shoes. The old lady had very poor[2] sight[3]. She did not know that the shoes were red, and bought them.

Karen wore them to her confirmation[4]. Everyone was quite[5] shocked to see her shoes. During her confirmation, Karen only thought about her pretty red shoes.

Later[6] that day, the old lady heard about the color of her shoes from a neighbor[7].

"Karen! It was very bad of you to wear red shoes to church. You must always wear black shoes," she scolded[8].

1. **confirm** [kən`fɜːrm] (v.) 施堅信禮
2. **poor** [pʊr] (a.) 不足的；貧困的
3. **sight** [saɪt] (n.) 視力
4. **confirmation**
   [ˌkɑːnfərˈmeɪʃən] (n.) 堅信禮
5. **quite** [kwaɪt] (adv.) 相當
6. **later** [ˈleɪtə(r)] (adv.) 較晚地
7. **neighbor** [ˈneɪbə(r)] (n.) 鄰居
8. **scold** [skoʊld] (v.) 責罵

🎧 25

The next Sunday, Karen looked at[1] her black shoes and then[2] at her red shoes. She put on her red ones. Karen and the old lady walked to church along[3] a dusty[4] road[5].

Outside[6] the church door, there was an old soldier[7] standing. "Shall I dust[8] your shoes for you?" he asked them.

"Yes, please do so," they replied[9].

The old soldier dusted them and said to Karen, "What pretty dancing shoes! Be careful[10] when you dance!"

Then he hit[11] the bottom[12] of her shoes with his hand.

1. **look at** 看
2. **then** [ðɛn] (adv.) 然後
3. **along** [ə`lɔːŋ] (prep.) 沿著
4. **dusty** [`dʌstɪ] (a.) 滿是灰塵的
5. **road** [roʊd] (n.) 道路
6. **outside** [`aʊt`saɪd] (prep.) 在……外面
7. **soldier** [`soʊldʒə(r)] (n.) 軍人；士兵
8. **dust** [dʌst] (v.) 除去灰塵
9. **reply** [rɪ`plaɪ] (v.) 回答
10. **careful** [`kɛrfəl] (a.) 小心的
11. **hit** [hɪt] (v.) 打 (hit-hit-hit)
12. **bottom** [`bɑːtəm] (n.) 底部

**One Point Lesson**

◦ **Shall I dust your shoes for you?** 我可以幫你擦皮鞋嗎？

**Shall I . . .** : 我可以……嗎？（詢問對方有何指示的客氣用法）

ex **Shall I take your coat?** 我可以幫你拿外套嗎？

77

After church[1], Karen started to get into[2] the carriage.

Just at that moment[3], the old soldier said to her again, "What pretty dancing shoes!"

When she heard that, she danced a few steps[4]. Then something very strange[5] happened[6]. She couldn't stop dancing. She danced all the way[7] around the church.

The coachman[8] grabbed[9] her and put her in the carriage. Her feet continued[10] to dance in the carriage. She even[11] kicked the old lady.

At last[12] they got the shoes off and put them away[13] in the cupboard[14]. But Karen loved those shoes.

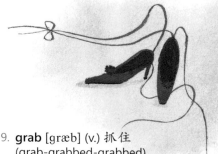

1. **after church** 做完禮拜後
2. **get into** 進入；上（車）
3. **just at that moment** 就在那個時刻
4. **step** [step] (n.) 腳步
5. **strange** [streɪndʒ] (a.) 奇怪的
6. **happen** [ˋhæpən] (v.) 發生
7. **all the way** 一路上
8. **coachman** [ˋkoutʃmæn] (n.) 馬車夫

9. **grab** [græb] (v.) 抓住 (grab-grabbed-grabbed)
10. **continue** [kənˋtɪnju:] (v.) 繼續
11. **even** [ˋi:vn] (adv.) 甚至
12. **at last** 最後
13. **put away** 丟到一邊
14. **cupboard** [ˋkʌbərd] (n.) 櫥櫃

**One Point Lesson**

When she heard that, she danced a few steps.
當她聽到那句話時，她跳了幾步。

**a few**：few 是指「幾乎沒有」，但 a few 是指「一些」（＝ some）。

ex I have a few English dictionaries.
我有一些英文字典。

**A** Fill in the blanks to complete the vocabulary.

**❶** not very strong ⇨ w ___ ___ ___

**❷** to bring up a child ⇨ r ___ ___ ___ ___

**❸** a ceremony for a dead person
⇨ f ___ ___ ___ ___ ___ ___

**❹** a vehicle which is pulled by horses
⇨ c ___ ___ ___ ___ ___ ___ ___

**❺** a queen or king's daughter
⇨ p ___ ___ ___ ___ ___ ___ ___

**B** Fill in the blanks with the given words.

along    behind    off    outside

**❶** Karen's mother died soon after. She was walking _____ her mother's coffin.

**❷** Karen and the old lady walked to church _____ a dusty road. _____ the church door, there was an old soldier standing.

**❸** Karen could not stop dancing. The coachman grabbed her and put her in the carriage. He got the shoes _____ and put them away in the cupboard.

## C Choose the correct answer.

**1** Why did the old lady buy Karen some red shoes?

(a) Because Karen needed red shoes for her confirmation.

(b) Because they were the cheapest shoes.

(c) Because she couldn't see the color correctly.

**2** What color shoes should Karen wear to church?

(a) very bright color

(b) very pale color

(c) very dark color

## D Rearrange the sentences in chronological order.

**1** Karen's mother died.

**2** Karen wore her red shoes to her confirmation.

**3** An old soldier dusted and hit Karen's red shoes.

**4** Karen went to live with the kind, old lady.

**5** An old shoe maker made a pair of red shoes for her.

_____ ⇨ _____ ⇨ _____ ⇨ _____ ⇨ _____

# Chapter Two

# 🎧27 The Evil[1] Shoes

Sometime later, the old lady became very sick[2]. Many people said she could not live. She needed a lot of[3] care[4]. Karen was the best[5] person to do this.

She took good care of her for a while[6]. One day, she received[7] an invitation[8] to a ball[9].

"A ball!" thought Karen. "I would love to [10] go." But then she thought of the old lady. "I must stay [11] here."

Soon after she changed her mind [12]. "But she's going to die anyway [13]. I'm going to the ball," decided the selfish [14] girl. She got dressed and put on her red dancing shoes.

1. **evil** [`ˋiːvəl] (a.) 邪惡的
2. **sick** [sɪk] (a.) 生病的
3. **a lot of** 很多
4. **care** [ker] (n.) 關懷
5. **the best** 最好的（well 的最高級）
6. **for a while** 一陣子
7. **receive** [rɪˋsiːv] (v.) 收到
8. **invitation** [ˌɪnvɪˋteɪʃn] (n.) 邀請函

9. **ball** [bɔːl] (n.) 舞會
10. **would love to** 很高興去
11. **stay** [steɪ] (v.) 待著；留下
12. **change one's mind**
    改變心意（mind：心）
13. **anyway** [`ˋeniweɪ] (adv.)
    無論如何；反正
14. **selfish** [`ˋselfɪʃ] (a.) 自私的

**One Point Lesson**

She is going to die anyway. 反正她快死了。

**be going to + 原形動詞**：用於未來式（ = will）是「快要⋯⋯；將要⋯⋯」的意思。

ex What are you going to do tonight?
你今晚要做什麼？

Karen went to the ball. She danced and danced. Then, the shoes started to do strange things. The shoes took Karen out[1] into the street and out of the town. She danced into a dark forest[2].

She tried to[3] stop[4], but she couldn't. Then, she heard a voice,

"They are such[5] pretty dancing shoes!" It was the old soldier.

She became extremely frightened[6]. She wanted to throw her shoes off[7]. But now it was too late[8]. She danced for days and for nights. She could never stop to rest[9].

1. **take A out** 帶 A 出去
2. **forest** [ˋfɔːrɪst] (n.) 森林
3. **try to** 試著去……
4. **stop** [staːp] (v.) 停止
   (stop-stopped-stopped)
5. **such** [sʌtʃ] (a.) 如此的
6. **frightened** [ˋfraɪtnd]
   (a.) 害怕的
7. **throw off** 扔掉
8. **late** [leɪt] (a.) 遲的
9. **rest** [rest] (v.) 休息

🎧 29

　　Karen danced toward the church door. At that moment, she saw an angel[1]. It was dressed in white and held[2] a big sword[3].

　　"Dance, you wicked[4] girl," he said. "Proud[5] people will see you. They will learn from your mistakes[6]."

1. **angel** [`eɪndʒl] (n.) 天使
2. **hold** [hoʊld] (v.) 握著
   (hold-held-held)
3. **sword** [sɔːrd] (n.) 劍
4. **wicked** [`wɪkɪd] (a.) 邪惡的
5. **proud** [praʊd] (a.)
   驕傲的；有自尊心的
6. **mistake** [mɪ`steɪk] (n.) 錯誤
7. **mercy** [`mɜːrsi] (n.) 慈悲
8. **beg** [beg] (v.) 懇求原諒
   (beg-begged-begged)
9. **churchyard** [`tʃɜːrtʃjɑːrd]
   (n.) 教堂庭院；墓園
10. **on and on** 不停地
11. **lonely** [`loʊnli] (a.) 孤獨的
12. **executioner** [ˌeksə`kjuːʃɪnə(r)]
    (n.) 劊子手
13. **cut off** 砍斷
14. **dance away** 跳著離去
15. **crutches** [`krʌtʃɪz] (n.) 枴杖

"Please have mercy[7] on me," Karen begged[8].

Karen didn't hear the angel reply. The shoes danced her out of the churchyard[9]. She danced on and on[10]. She came to a small, lonely[11] house. It was an executioner's[12] house.

She called out, "Please cut off[13] my feet. They are wearing red dancing shoes."

She told him about all her sins and then the man cut off her feet. She watched the red shoes dance away[14] with her feet.

The executioner made two wooden feet and crutches[15] for her.

"I will go to church now," she told him.

## 30

Karen went to a church and begged to the parson[1], "Please let[2] me live with you. I will work hard[3] and be a good person."

Karen lived in the parson's house. She read the Bible[4] and took care of many children. She whole-heartedly[5] repented[6].

One Sunday, she heard a sound. It was the sound of church music.

She cried out[7] to God, "Dear[8] God, please forgive[9] me!"

At that moment, the room became very bright[10]. There was an angel standing before her.

1. **parson** [`pɑːrsn]
   (n.) 教區牧師
2. **let** [let] (v.) 讓；使
   (let-let-let)
3. **hard** [hɑːrd] (adv.) 努力地
4. **the Bible** 聖經
5. **whole-heartedly**
   [ˌhoul`hɑːrtɪdli]
   (adv.) 全心全意地
6. **repent** [rɪ`pent] (v.) 悔改
7. **cry out** 大聲呼喊
8. **dear** [dɪr] (a.) 親愛的
9. **forgive** [fər`gɪv] (v.) 原諒
   (forgive-forgave-forgiven)
10. **bright** [braɪt] (a.) 明亮的

Please let me live with you.
請讓我跟你一起住。

---

**let + somebody + 原形動詞：讓某人做某事**

ex I'll let you know my email address.
我會讓你知道我的電子郵件地址。

1. **same** [seɪm] (a.) 相同的
2. **bunch** [bʌntʃ] (n.) 束；串
3. **instead of** 代替；而不是⋯⋯
4. **touch** [tʌtʃ] (v.) 觸摸
5. **organ** [ˋɔːrgən] (n.) 風琴
6. **play** [pleɪ] (v.) 彈奏

7. **glad** [glæd] (a.) 高興的
8. **speak of** 說到；提到
9. **peace** [piːs] (n.) 和平
10. **joy** [dʒɔɪ] (n.) 喜樂

*The Red Shoes*

## 31

It was the same[1] angel she saw in the churchyard. This time he was different. He had a bunch[2] of roses instead of[3] the sword.

He touched[4] her room with the roses. Her room became the church. She could hear the organ[5] playing[6].

People said to her, "It is good to see you, Karen. We are glad[7] that you came."

No one ever spoke of[8] the red shoes again. Karen started to have a feeling of peace[9] and joy[10].

---

**One Point Lesson**

• **No one ever spoke of the red shoes again.**
再也沒有人提到紅舞鞋了。

---

**no . . . ever**：再也沒有……。not ever = never

ex **No one ever goes that road.**
再也沒有人走那條路了。

**A** Fill in blanks with the correct form of the given words.

**1** One day Karen received an _____ (invite) to a ball.

**2** The _____ (self) girl decided to go to the ball.

**3** She got _____ (dress) and put on her _____ (dance) shoes.

**B** Fill in blanks with the given words.

to    off    out    into    out of

Karen went _____ the ball. She danced and danced. Then, the shoes started to do strange things. The shoes took Karen _____ into the street and _____ the town. She danced _____ a dark forest. She tried to stop but she couldn't. Then, she heard a voice, "They are such pretty dancing shoes!" It was the old soldier. She became extremely frightened. She tried to throw her shoes _____ , but it was too late.

## C True or False.

T F ❶ Karen only danced when the sun was shining.

T F ❷ The angel spoke very seriously to Karen.

T F ❸ The parson made her two new feet.

T F ❹ Karen went to the parson's house and lived with his family.

T F ❺ In the end, God forgave all of Karen's sins.

## D Rearrange the sentences in chronological order.

❶ Karen went to live at the Parson's house.

❷ The Angel appeared with a bunch of roses.

❸ Karen danced past the executioner's house.

❹ Karen read the Bible and took care of many children.

❺ Karen went to enjoy herself at the ball.

_____ ⇨ _____ ⇨ _____ ⇨ _____ ⇨ _____

# Appendixes

# 1  Basic Grammar

要增強英文閱讀理解能力，應練習找出英文的主結構。
要擁有良好的英語閱讀能力，首先要理解英文的段落結構。

## 「英文的主要句型結構比較簡單」

所有的英語文章都是由主詞和動詞所構成的，無論文章再怎麼長或複雜，它的架構一定是「主詞和動詞」，而「補語」和「受詞」是做補充主詞和動詞的角色。

| 主詞 | 動詞 |
|------|------|
| 某樣東西 | 如何做 |
| 人、事、物 | |

He  runs  (very fast).

他　　跑　（非常快）

It  is raining .

雨　正在下

| 主詞 | 動詞 | 補語 |
|------|------|------|
| 某樣東西 | 如何做 | 怎麼樣 |
| 人、事、物 | | |

補充的話

This  is  a cat .

這　　是　一隻貓。

The cat  is  very  big .

那隻貓　是 非常　大

主詞　　動詞　　受詞

某樣東西　如何做　　　什麼
人、事、物

人，事物，
兩者皆是受詞

I  like  you .　　　　　　You  gave  me  some flowers .

我 喜歡 你。　　　　　　你　 給　 我　　 一些花

主詞　　動詞　　受詞　　補語

某樣東西　如何做　　什麼　怎麼樣／什麼
人、事、物

You  make  me  happy .　　I  saw  him  running .

你 使（讓）我 幸福（快樂） 我 看到　 他　 跑

　　其他修飾語或副詞等，都可以視為為了完成句子而臨時、額外、特別附加的，閱讀起來便可更加輕鬆；先具備這些基本概念，再閱讀《賣火柴的小女孩》的部分精選篇章，最後做了解文章整體架構的練習。

A shape  moved  through the dark streets.

一個人影　 移動　 穿越　 黑暗的街道

It  was  terribly  cold  and  It  was snowing .

它　是 非常地　 冷　 而且 它　 正在下雪

The shape  slowly  came  closer.  It  was  a little girl .

那個人影　 慢慢地　來 愈來愈近 它 是 一個小女孩

Her clothes  were  dirty , and  she  had  no shoes .

她的衣服　　是　 髒的 而且 她　　 沒有鞋子

97

The little girl walked in the snow with bare feet.
這小女孩 走路 在雪中 赤腳

In her hands, she was carrying some matches .
在她手裡 她 帶了 一些火柴

Every day, she went out to sell matches.
每天 她 出去 賣火柴

But today she didn't sell any .
但 今天 她 沒有 賣出 任何東西

She was so cold but she couldn't go home.
她 是 如此 冷 但是 她 不能 回 家

When she didn't sell any matches, her father would beat her .
當 她 沒有賣出 火柴時 她的父親 會 打 她

On this terrible day, she found a corner and sat down .
在這個惡劣的天氣 她 找到 一個角落 並 坐下

She tried to warm herself . But she only became colder .
她 試著 讓自己溫暖 但是 她 只是 變得 更冷

Her body was like ice.
她的身體 是 像冰

She rubbed her hands together to make them warm.
她 摩擦 她的手 一起 以便讓手溫暖

It was useless .
它 是 沒用的

"Ah! The matches," she thought .
啊， 火柴 她 想到

"Just one! It will make my hands warmer ."
只要一根 它 將 使 我的手 暖一些

She took one match and struck it against the wall.

她 拿 一根火柴 並 點 它 在牆上

She was amazed.

她 是 吃驚的

"Oh, it is so beautiful !" she thought.

啊 它 是 如此 美麗 她 想

She felt the warmth from that one tiny match.

她 感覺 溫暖 從那根小火柴

A little girl named Karen lived with her mother.

一個小女孩 名叫凱倫 住 和她母親

She was a small and weak-looking girl.

她 是 看起來很瘦小、很虛弱的小女孩

In summer she never had any shoes because she was very poor.

在夏天 她 從來沒有 鞋 因為她很窮

In winter she had to wear a pair of heavy wooden shoes.

在冬天 她 必須 穿 一雙厚重的木鞋

These shoes always made her feet hurt.

這雙鞋 總是 讓 她的腳 痛

But she didn't have anything else to wear.

但是 她 沒有 別的東西可以穿

An old shoemaker in the village felt sorry for her

一個老鞋匠 在村子裡 感到 難過 為她

and made a pair of red shoes for her.

並 做了 一雙紅鞋 給她

They weren't very good shoes, but they made her very happy.

它們 不是 非常好的鞋子 但 它們 使 她 非常 快樂

# Guide to Listening Comprehension

 Use your book's CD to enjoy the audio version. When listening to the story, use some of the techniques shown below. If you take time to study some phonetic characteristics of English, listening will be easier.

## *Get in the flow of English.*

English creates a rhythm formed by combinations of strong and weak stress intonations. Each word has its particular stress that combines with other words to form the overall pattern of stress or rhythm in a particular sentence.

When speaking and listening to English, it is essential to get in the flow of the rhythm of English. It takes a lot of practice to get used to such a rhythm. So, you need to start by identifying the stressed syllable in a word.

## Listen for the strongly stressed words and phrases.

In English, key words and phrases that are essential to the meaning of a sentence are stressed louder. Therefore, pay attention to the words stressed with a higher pitch. When listening to an English recording for the first time, what matters most is to listen for a general understanding of what you hear. Do not try to hear every single word. Most of the unstressed words are articles or auxiliary verbs, which don't play an important role in the general context. At this level, you can ignore them.

## Pay attention to liaisons.

In reading English, words are written with a space between them. There isn't such an obvious guide when it comes to listening to English. In oral English, there are many cases when the sounds of words are linked with adjacent words.

For instance, let's think about the phrase "**take off**," which can be used in "take off your clothes." "Take off your clothes" doesn't sound like [teɪk ɔːf] with each of the words completely and clearly separated from the others. Instead, it sounds as if almost all the words in context are slurred together, [ˈteɪkɔːf], for a more natural sound.

## Shadow the voice of the native speaker.

Finally, you need to mimic the voice of the native speaker. Once you are sure you know how to pronounce all the words in a sentence, try to repeat them like an echo. Listen to the book again, but this time you should try a fun exercise while listening to the English.

This exercise is called "shadowing." The word "shadow" means a dark shade that is formed on a surface. When used as a verb, the word refers to the action of following someone or something like a shadow. In this exercise, pretend you are a parrot and try to shadow the voice of the native speaker.

Try to mimic the reader's voice by speaking at the same speed, with the same strong and weak stresses on words, and pausing or stopping at the same points.

Experts have already proven this technique to be effective. If you practice this shadowing exercise, your English speaking and listening skills will improve by leaps and bounds. While shadowing the native speaker, don't forget to pay attention to the meaning of each phrase and sentence.

Listen to what you want to shadow many times. Start out by just trying to shadow a few words or a sentence.

 Mimic the CD out loud. You can shadow everything the speaker says as if you are singing a round, or you also can speak simultaneously with the recorded voice of the native speaker.

 As you practice more, try to shadow more. For instance, shadow a whole sentence or paragraph instead of just a few words.

# Listening Guide

以下為《賣火柴的小女孩》各章節的前半部。一開始若能聽清楚發音，之後就沒有聽力的負擔。先聽過摘錄的章節，之後再反覆聆聽括弧內單字的發音，並仔細閱讀各種發音的說明。以下都是以英語的典型發音為基礎，所做的簡易說明，即使這裡未提到的發音，也可以配合音檔反覆聆聽，如此一來聽力必能更上層樓。

## The Little Match Girl

**Chapter One** page 16

A shape moved through the dark ( **1** ). It was terribly cold and it ( **2** ) ( ). The shape slowly came closer. It was a little girl. Her clothes were ( **3** ), and she had no shoes. Some time ago she had slippers. Unfortunately, she ( **4** ) ( ). Her shoes were once her mother's. But they were so big. One day, when she was ( **5** ) ( ) a street, they fell off. The snow was falling from the ( **6** ) winter sky. It was New Year's Eve. The streets were ( **7** ) empty now.

**❶ streets:** 無聲子音 p、t、k 接在 s- 後面，會變成有聲子音，變成 [b]、[d]、[g]。

**❷ was snowing:** was 和 snowing 連在一起發音時，was 的 [s] 會和 snowing 的 [s] 連在一起，只發一個 [s] 的音，成為 wasnowing。

**❸ dirty:** dirty 的 t 在 ir [ɜːr] 後面，聽起來變成像是 d 的音。

**❹ lost them:** lost 在和 them 一起念時，字尾的 t 會和 them 的 th 合在一起，發出類似 los-them 的音。通常 them 在口語中，th 的音會省略，只會發出 'em。

**❺ running across:** running 和 across 連在一起時，across 前面的 a- 會消失，而發成 cross。

**❻ beautiful:** 重音在第一音節，ti 是發 [tə] 的音，但因為不是重音，所以會輕輕唸成像 r 帶過。

**❼ almost:** almost 的重音在第一音節，字尾 st 兩個子音連在一起，聽起來是輕柔短促的摩擦音。

## The Emperor's New Clothes

**Chapter One** page 42 🎧33

A long time ago, there ( ❶ ) ( ) emperor.
( ❷ ) ( ) love was his clothes. Every day, he wore the finest clothes. He often changed a few times a day. His purpose was always to show off his clothes. When he met people from other countries, he cared only about his clothes. Two thieves ( ❸ ) ( ) this emperor. They ( ❹ ) ( ) a plan to deceive the emperor.

❶ **lived an:** lived 字尾的 d 音，會和 an 連起來，變成 live-dan 的音。

❷ **The emperor's:** emperor 的重音在第一音節，由於第一個音是母音 [e]，所以前面的 the 要發成 [ði]。

❸ **heard about:** about 的重音在第二音節，所以 a 輕輕地和前面的 heard 連在一起，變成 hearda-bout 的音。

❹ **thought of:** thought 字尾的 t 和 of 連在一起，會變成 d，因此聽起來像是 though-dav。注意 of 字尾發有聲子音 [v]。

## The Red Shoes

A little girl named Karen lived with her mother. She was a ( ❶ ) ( ) ( )-looking girl. In summer she never had any shoes because she was very poor. In winter she ( ❷ ) ( ) wear a pair of heavy wooden shoes. These shoes always ( ❸ ) ( ) feet hurt. But she ( ❹ ) have anything else to wear.

❶ **small and weak**: and 在兩個字中間通常會發成 n 的音，變成 small-n-weak。

❷ **had to**: had 和 to 連在一起，had 的 d 會消失，變成 ha-to 的音。

❸ **made her**: her / him / he / his 前面的 h，在連音時經常會省略。因此 made her 會發成類似 made-er 的音。

❹ **didn't**: didn't 重音在第一音節，字尾的 t 很輕，幾乎聽不見。

# 4

# Listening Comprehension

**A** Listen to the CD and choose the correct answer.

1. Every day, the emperor (were / wore) the finest clothes.

2. The little girl (lifted / left) her hands toward the Christmas tree.

3. When they were alone, the two thieves (left and left / laughed and laughed).

4. The angel was dressed in white and (had / held) a big sword.

5. The shoes (danced her / then set her) out of the churchyard.

**B** True or False.

| | | |
|---|---|---|
| T F | 1 | .............................................. |
| T F | 2 | .............................................. |
| T F | 3 | .............................................. |
| T F | 4 | .............................................. |
| T F | 5 | .............................................. |
| T F | 6 | .............................................. |
| T F | 7 | .............................................. |

# C Listen to the CD and choose the correct answer.

**1** _____?

(a) A big goose.

(b) A stove.

(c) A Christmas tree.


**2** _____?

(a) To ask them to make new clothes with the magic cloth.

(b) To show off his finest clothes.

(c) To make them help him when he changed his clothes.


**3** _____?

(a) To buy her a pair of red shoes.

(b) To take her to the castle to see the princess.

(c) To raise and take care of her.


**4** _____?

(a) The room changed into a church.

(b) She suddenly stopped dancing.

(c) She was out in a dark forest.

# Translation

## 作者簡介

p.4 1805年4月2日，漢斯·克里斯汀·安徒生出生於歐登塞菲英島上的一個小漁村，父親是個窮鞋匠。不過父親喜愛文學、思想先進，他自己喜歡閱讀，也鼓勵兒子安徒生培養自己的文藝興趣。

安徒生在大學時代開始寫作，他的第一本小說《即興詩人》（*The Improvisatore*），以自己1833年在義大利的旅遊經歷為題材，這本小說佳評如潮，享有的聲譽甚至更勝於他的第一部童話故事《講給孩子們聽的故事》（*Tales Told for Children*）。後來，安徒生成為深受喜愛的兒童文學作家。1875年，安徒生辭世，出版的故事共計一百三十餘則。

安徒生的許多著作被視為是最優異的兒童文學作品，例如《美人魚》（*The Little Mermaid*）、《醜小鴨》（*The Ugly Duckling*）、《國王的新衣》（*The Emperor's New Clothes*）。儘管遭遇諸多困難，安徒生克服了各種挑戰，成為成功的作家。安徒生在作品中熱衷於透過抒情詩意的筆觸，來展現美麗虛幻的幻想世界和人道主義。

安徒生過著獨居生活，並於1875年孤獨離世。在他的出殯日，丹麥舉國上下都穿著喪服，國王和皇后並親赴葬禮。安徒生也是一位活躍的詩人，而他美麗的童話故事仍受到世界各地人們的喜愛。

## 賣火柴的小女孩

**p. 5** 除夕夜裡，一位貧窮的小女孩走在白雪覆蓋的街道上。今天一整天，她連一盒火柴都沒有賣出去，所以不敢回家。可憐的賣火柴小女孩難過地坐在噴泉池邊，她掏出一根火柴，將火柴點燃並用手圍住火光，就在此時，她在火光中看到了不可思議的東西……

就像安徒生的許多故事一樣，世界各地的大人小孩都被《賣火柴的小女孩》所觸動。作者是因為自己的媽媽而寫了這個故事，他媽媽的童年生活一貧如洗。

## 國王的新衣

這個故事改編自十四世紀西班牙作家曼紐爾（J. Manuel）的作品《盧卡諾爾伯爵》（*Duke Rukanore*）。從前，有一位國王因為非常著迷於新衣服，可以為新衣服一擲千金。有一天，幾個騙子唬弄國王說，他們能夠製作一種衣服，那是愚笨的人所看不到的衣服。原著故事用了批判性的眼光來看社會。

## 紅舞鞋

很久以前，有一位出身貧窮的美麗小女孩，她平時只能打赤腳。後來，她買了一雙新的紅鞋，但是她只要一穿上紅鞋，就會止不住地跳舞。有一天，小女孩的養母生病了，但是她不但沒有照顧媽媽，還穿上紅鞋去參加舞會，開始跳起舞來。奇怪的是，她無法脫下鞋子，只好一直跳到遠處的陰暗林子裡，在那裡跳了幾天幾夜。這個故事有強烈的基督教意味：對自私自利的懲罰。

## 賣火柴的小女孩

## [第一章] 女孩和一根火柴

**p. 16** 有一個人影沿著黑暗的街道移動。天氣冷得不得了，而且還在下雪。慢慢地那個人影愈來愈近。是個小女孩。

她的衣服髒兮兮的，腳上沒有穿鞋。不久之前她還有拖鞋穿，但不幸的是，拖鞋不見了。她的鞋子是她媽媽的，但鞋子太大了。就在某一天，當她跑過街道時，鞋子掉了。

**p. 18** 雪從冬天美麗的天空落下。那天正是除夕。此時街上幾乎空空蕩蕩的，大家都回到自己溫暖的家中。

這個小女孩赤腳走在雪中，她的手上帶著一些火柴；每天，她都外出去賣火柴，但是今天她一根也沒賣出去。她覺得很冷，可是她不能回家；因為只要她火柴沒賣掉，她爸爸就會打她。

**p. 20** 「噢！我好餓，」她說。「我想吃東西。我也很冷，」她在腦子裡想著。

她走過幾棟房子，透過窗戶，她可以看到裡面燈火通明。然後，她聞到烤肉的香味，這讓她覺得很難熬，她真在太餓了。

「我想吃那個好吃的肉，」她想。「好多人正在跟家人愉快地共度佳節，享受佳餚。」

**p. 22** 在這個惡劣的天候下,她找到了一處角落坐下來,她試著讓自己溫暖,結果卻只是更冷。她的身體像冰一樣冷,她摩擦雙手取暖,但是沒有用。

「啊!火柴,」她想到。「只要一根!就能讓我的手變暖。」她拿出一根火柴,往牆上劃了一下,她感到很驚奇。

「啊!真漂亮!」她想。

這根小小的火柴,讓她感到溫暖。

**p. 25** 突然間,一切都變得很奇怪。小女孩變成在另一個地方,她面前有一個大火爐。

「這是什麼?」她問道。「這個爐子好溫暖。」

她感覺到這個美妙的爐子傳來的溫暖。

「我要永遠待在這兒。」

她把手再往火爐移近。一瞬間,這一切都消失了。她看著她的手,手裡是燒完的火柴。她覺得很失望。

## [第二章] 天堂之旅

**p. 28** 「我要再點一根火柴,」她想著。「或許火爐會再出現。」

再一次,火柴在冰冷的夜空中,如鑽石般發出光芒。這次景象完全不同。她看到一間很棒的房間。

「噢，真是太美妙了！」她大叫。

裡面有雅緻的家具，桌上放滿了美味的大餐，中間擺了一隻肥鵝，香味讓人垂涎三尺。

`p. 30–31` 小女孩看著這所有的一切。

「我想吃美味的食物，」她想著。「我想坐在高雅的椅子上。」

突然，那隻鵝滾向了可憐的小女孩。她試著去拿，但牠消失得無影無蹤了，只剩下那根燒過的火柴。

她想都沒想，立即再拿出一根來點上，因為她想要再看看那個美妙的景象。

這回，她坐在最令人嘆為觀止的聖誕樹下。這一幕比其他景象更棒。

`p. 32–33` 她想觸摸其中一根蠟燭。她把手伸向樹，但是所有蠟燭都往上飛，飛得愈來愈高，最後變成了星星。她看到其中一顆星星落下，在天空劃出火一般的線條。

這時小女孩想起了奶奶。奶奶在很多年前過世了，她是唯一善待小女孩的人。

「某個地方有人死了，」她低語。「奶奶告訴我的。當星星從天空落下時，那個人的靈魂就會上天堂。」

p. 34–35 她覺得很悲傷。她非常想念她奶奶。她立刻再點上一根火柴,這次比之前點的火柴還要亮。

她看著火光的中心,慢慢地,她奶奶的人影出現了,她的臉看起來非常和藹慈祥。

「奶奶!」她大叫。「我好想你,你不在我身邊我很難過,請帶我跟你一起走。火柴熄滅後,你不要消失,我不要你再離開我了。」

p. 36 然後小女孩想出了一個辦法。她把剩下的火柴都點上了,火柴的光芒燦爛奪目。

奶奶抱著小女孩,小女孩感到很安全,因為現在有她奶奶在身邊了。他們在空中愈飛愈高,奶奶帶著小女孩到天堂去了。

在那個地方,小女孩再也不覺得冷,也不再感到飢餓或悲傷。她可以和慈愛的奶奶快樂地住在一起。

## 國王的新衣

## [第一章] 兩個小偷

p. 42–43 很久以前,有一位國王,這個國王的愛好就是他的衣服。他每天都穿著最好的衣服,一天常要換好幾次

衣服，目的不外乎炫耀自己的衣服。當他會見外賓時，他只關心自己的穿著。

　　兩個小偷聽説這個國王的事了，他們想出了一個計謀要欺騙國王。

　　「我們到那個城市去，我們可以假裝會織神奇的布料。」其中一個小偷説。

p. 44–45 兩個小偷來到了這個城市。

　　「我們會織神奇的布。愚人看不到這塊布，」他們説。不久，大家都聽説了神奇的布。連國王也聽到這件事了。

　　「神奇的布！」他想。「只有聰明人才看得見這塊布，而且人們都説它很漂亮。如果我用這塊布來做衣服，那我就能知道誰聰明、誰愚笨。我也能知道我的顧問大臣之中，哪些是有智慧的。」

p. 46–47 國王召那兩個騙子到宮裡來。「你們能不能用神奇的布幫我做出最棒的衣服？」國王問他們。

　　「當然可以啊，陛下。但是我們需要一大筆錢，還有絲料和金線。」

國王就給他們所有需要的東西。

他們很快就開始織神奇的布。

他們坐在織布機前面假裝在織布。他們擺動手臂，一副在縫衣服的樣子。

p. 48 幾天過後，國王漸漸好奇起來。

「不知道我的衣服是什麼樣子？」他想。

他叫來其中一位顧問大臣，對他說，「我要你去看看我的新衣服，然後立刻回來告訴我衣服的樣子。」

那位顧問大臣進入房間，告訴那兩個小偷，「我來看國王的新衣。」

「是的，是的，」他們熱絡地說，「這邊請。」

他們假裝拿起一些布。

「你覺得如何？很漂亮吧？」他們問。

p. 51 顧問大臣非常震驚，因為他根本沒看到任何東西。

他很擔心，「我很愚笨嗎？」他自忖。「不能讓任何人知道我看不到布。」

「啊，是的，很……很漂亮，」他說話的聲音很緊張。「顏色很鮮艷，國王一定會很高興的。」

顧問大臣回去見國王說，「那是我見過最上等的布料，你一定會對它很滿意。」

## ［第二章］ 國王穿新衣

p.54-55 國王愈來愈不耐煩，他決定親自去拜訪那兩個小偷。

　　他召集了很多皇室大臣們，大家都一起去看那兩個壞蛋。

　　在進門前，國王非常興奮。現在他左看右看，卻什麼都沒看到。

　　他心中忽然升起一種可怕的感覺，「我沒看到衣服，我很愚笨嗎？一定是。但我不能讓大臣們知道我看不見衣服。」

p.56-57 國王忽然驚呼，「這塊布是我見過最美的布。織布工！請加快腳步完成我的新衣。我希望能很快就穿上新裝。」

　　所有大臣點頭稱是，「對，這塊布很美，穿在你身上一定很好看，陛下。」

　　「我們很高興你滿意這塊布，」那兩個壞蛋說。

　　「我們會加緊努力，做出最美的衣裳。另外，我們還需要更多的錢、絲料和金線。」

　　等大家都走了，只剩他們兩個人時，他們笑個不停。

p. 58 最後這兩個人終於說，「完成了。」

國王非常高興，去看他的新衣。兩個壞蛋站立著，雙手在空中比劃，看起來好像拿著什麼東西似的。其實當然沒有東西。

「這件衣服是不是很棒？質地非常輕，事實上，你甚至會以為你沒穿衣服呢，」他們說。

國王把自己的衣服脫掉，那兩個小偷假裝幫他穿上新衣。

p. 60–61 國王在鏡子前不停轉身，說道，「這是我穿過最舒服的衣服，我很喜歡這件新衣。」

所有隨從都同意。當然，他們看到的只有他身上的內衣！

那天，有一場特別的慶典，所有人都在準備這個盛會。他的隨從假裝拉起他斗篷後面的下擺，國王趾高氣昂地走著。

p. 62–63 街上群眾圍觀並大喊，「衣服好漂亮！國王看起來真棒！」

然後，人群中有一個小孩子說，「爸爸，國王沒穿衣服。」

所有人面面相覷，大家都知道沒有衣服。

人群中出現了竊竊私語，「國王沒穿衣服。」

國王全都聽見了，他也開始覺得很不好意思。他真的沒有穿衣服。

次日，再也沒有人提到國王的新衣，而且國王對衣著也不那麼招搖了。

## 紅舞鞋

## ［第一章］貧窮的小女孩

p. 68–69 有一個小女孩叫做凱倫，跟母親住在一起。她長得很瘦小，外表很虛弱。

她夏天時都不穿鞋子，因為家裡很窮。冬天時，她就得穿厚重的木鞋。

那雙鞋子常會讓她的腳痛，但她沒有其他鞋子可以穿。

村子裡的一個老鞋匠覺得她很可憐，就做了一雙紅鞋給她。這雙鞋質料並不是很好，但是小女孩非常開心。

p. 70–71 不幸地，小女孩的母親不久就過世了。在她母親的喪禮上，她第一次穿上那雙新的紅鞋。凱倫走在她母親的靈柩後面。

這時有一輛大馬車經過，馬車裡的一位老太太看到這個小女孩，立即對她產生憐憫之心。

因此她就對教堂牧師說，「把她交給我吧，我會撫養、照顧她。」

凱倫認為這都是因為那雙紅鞋的關係，但是老太太說，「那雙鞋很可怕，把它丟掉吧。」

p. 73 凱倫就去和老太太一起住。她每天都穿好的吃好的，也學了很多東西，她變成了一個非常漂亮的女孩。

有一天，皇后和她的女兒一起出遊，所有村民都擠到附近的城堡去看他們，凱倫也去了。

透過窗戶，她可以看到那位公主，她身穿白衣，和一雙漂亮
的紅鞋。然後，凱倫就想起她以前那雙舊紅鞋。

**p. 74** 凱倫長大了，行堅信禮的時候到了。參加堅信禮，她需要
新衣和新鞋。

在商店裡，凱倫找到了像公主穿的紅鞋，但是她得穿黑鞋。
老太太的視力很差，她不知道那雙鞋是紅色的，就買下來了。

凱倫穿著那雙紅鞋去受堅信禮，每個人看到她的鞋子都很訝
異。在堅信禮的過程中，凱倫只想到她的漂亮紅鞋。

那天稍晚，老太太從鄰居那裡聽說那雙鞋子是紅色的。

「凱倫！你真壞，竟然穿紅鞋去教堂。你一定要穿黑鞋去才
行，」老太太責罵她。

**p. 76** 隔週週日，凱倫望著她
的黑鞋，然後又看看她的紅鞋，
最後她穿上了紅鞋。凱倫和老太
太經過一條滿是塵土的路，才走
到教堂。

在教堂門口，站了一位老
兵。「我可以幫你擦掉鞋子上
的塵土嗎？」他問他們兩個。

「可以，麻煩你了，」他們回答。

那個老兵擦了鞋子，然後對凱倫說，「好漂亮的舞鞋！你跳
舞的時候要小心一點！」

然後他用手在鞋底打了一下。

**p.78–79** 做完禮拜後，凱倫上了馬車。

就在這個時刻，那位老兵又對她說，「好漂亮的舞鞋！」

當她聽到這句話時，她立刻跳了幾步。然後奇怪的事就發生了，她沒辦法停止跳舞，她沿著教堂四周不停地跳。

馬車夫抓住她，把她拉進馬車裡。她在馬車上腳還是不停地跳著，甚至還踢到了老太太。

最後他們終於把鞋子脫掉，放進了櫥櫃裡。但是凱倫還是很喜歡那雙鞋。

## [ 第二章 ] 邪惡的鞋子

p. 82–83 過了一陣子，老太太身體愈來愈不行了，很多人都說她活不了了，她需要有人好好照顧她，而凱倫就是最佳人選。

她悉心照料老太太好一陣子，有一天，她收到一張舞會的邀請函。

「舞會！」凱倫想。「我好想去參加。」但她想到了老太太，「我必須留在這裡。」

沒多久她就改變主意了，「不過反正她快死了，我要去參加舞會，」這個自私的女孩下定決心了，於是她穿著打扮好，並穿上她的紅舞鞋。

p. 84 凱倫去了舞會，她不斷地跳著舞。然後，鞋子開始出現了奇怪的狀況。鞋子帶著凱倫跳到街上，還出了城鎮，跳著進入了黑暗的森林。

她想停下來，但停不下來。然後她聽到了一個聲音。

「這雙舞鞋真漂亮！」是那位老兵。

她感覺極度害怕，她想把鞋子丟掉，但現在已經太遲了。她從白天跳到夜晚，無法停下來休息。

p. 86–87 凱倫一路跳到了教堂門口。就在那時，她看到了一位天使，天使一身白衣，手持長劍。

「跳吧，你這個邪惡的女孩，」他說。「驕傲的人會看見你，然後就會從你的錯誤中學到教訓。」

「請憐憫我。」凱倫懇求。

凱倫沒有聽到天使的回音，鞋子就帶著她跳出了教堂庭院。她不停地跳著，來到了一間偏僻的小房子，那是劊子手住的地方。

她大叫，「請砍斷我的腳，我的腳穿著紅舞鞋。」

她跟劊子手訴說她所有的罪惡，然後劊子手就砍斷了她的腳。她看著紅舞鞋繼續帶著她的腳跳走了。

劊子手幫她做了兩隻木腳，和一根枴杖。

「我現在要去教堂，」她告訴劊子手。

p. 89 凱倫到了教堂，向牧師乞求，「請讓我跟你住在一起。我會努力工作，當一個好人。」

凱倫就住在牧師的家裡，她每天讀聖經，照顧很多孩子。她全心全意地悔改了。

在某個星期天時，她聽到了一個聲音，那是教堂的音樂聲。

她對上帝呼喊，「親愛的上帝，請原諒我！」

就在那一刻，房間充滿了光明，有一個天使站著她面前。

p. 90 這位天使就是她在教堂庭院見到的天使，只是這次他不一樣了；他拿的不是劍，而是一束玫瑰花。

他用玫瑰花碰觸了她的房間，房間就變成了教堂，她還聽到風琴彈奏的聲音。

大家對她說，「看到你真好，凱倫。我們很高興你來了。」

沒有人再提起那雙紅鞋了，凱倫開始有了平安喜樂的感覺。

# Answers

P. 26   **A**   **1** tiny   **2** dirty   **3** empty   **4** warm

      **B**   **1** sell   **2** bare   **3** rubbed
             **4** stove   **5** gone

P. 27   **C**   **1 3 4** match   **2** corner

      **D**   **1** c   **2** b

P. 38   **A**   **1** Delicious   **2** disappears   **3** candle
             **4** heaven

      **B**   **1** F   **2** T   **3** F   **4** T   **5** F

P. 52   **A**   **1** clothes   **2** palace   **3** thief   **4** silk

      **B**   **1** T   **2** F   **3** T   **4** F

P. 53   **C**   **1** finest   **2** wise   **3** stupid

      **D**   **2** → **5** → **3** → **1** → **4**

P. 64   **A**   **1** impatient   **2** excited   **3** extremely
             **4** proudly

      **B**   **3** → **2** → **1** → **5** → **4**

P. 80   **A**   **1** weak   **2** raise   **3** funeral
             **4** carriage   **5** princess

      **B**   **1** behind   **2** along, Outside   **3** off

P. 81　Ⓒ　❶ c　❷ c

Ⓓ　❺ → ❶ → ❹ → ❷ → ❸

P. 92　Ⓐ　❶ invitation　❷ selfish　❸ dressed, dancing

Ⓑ　❶ to, out, out of, into, off

P. 93　Ⓒ　❶ F　❷ T　❸ F　❹ T　❺ T

Ⓓ　❺ → ❸ → ❶ → ❹ → ❷

P. 108　Ⓐ　❶ wore　❷ lifted　❸ laughed and laughed
　　　　　❹ held　❺ danced her

Ⓑ　❶ The little girl walked in the snow with no shoes. (T)
　　❷ When the match went out, everything was gone. (T)
　　❸ The emperor couldn't see the cloth because he was foolish. (F)
　　❹ Only a little child in the crowd could see the clothes. (F)
　　❺ It was bad to wear red shoes to church. (T)
　　❻ The angel helped Karen stop dancing. (F)
　　❼ Karen truly repented and begged for mercy. (T)

P. 109　Ⓒ　❶ When the little girl first lit a match, what did she watch? (b)
　　　　　❷ Why did the emperor call the two thieves to his palace? (a)
　　　　　❸ What did the old lady decide to do when she saw Karen at the funeral? (c)
　　　　　❹ What happened when the angel touched Karen's room with roses? (a)

國家圖書館出版品預行編目資料

賣火柴的小女孩【二版】/ Hans Christian
Andersen 著；Louise Benette, David Hwang
改寫. —二版. —[臺北市]：寂天文化, 2019.4 面 ;
公分. 中英對照

ISBN    978-986-318-796-7 (25K平裝附光碟片)
1.英語 2.讀本

805.18                          108005524

# 賣 火 柴 的 小 女 孩【二版】
## *The Little Match Girl*

作者 _ 安徒生
　　　（Hans Christian Andersen）
改寫 _ Louise Benette, David Hwang
插圖 _ Kim Hyeon-Jeong
翻譯 / 編輯 _ 李怡萍
校對 _ 申文怡
封面設計 _ 林書玉
播音員 _ Rebecca Kelly, Michael Blunk
製程管理 _ 洪巧玲

發行人 _ 周均亮
出版者 _ 寂天文化事業股份有限公司
電話 _ +886-2-2365-9739
傳真 _ +886-2-2365-9835
網址 _ www.icosmos.com.tw
讀者服務 _ onlineservice@icosmos.com.tw
出版日期 _ 2019年4月 二版一刷（250201）
郵撥帳號 _ 1998620-0 寂天文化事業股份有限公司

Adaptors

David Hwang

Michigan State University (MA, TESOL)
Ewha Womans University, English Chief Instructor,
CEO at EDITUS

Louise Benette

Macquarie University (MA, TESOL)
Sookmyung Women's University, English Instructor